Robin Hoodie

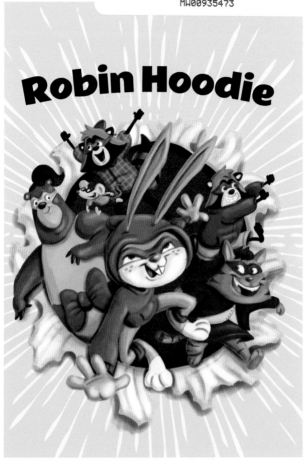

By Vickie An
Illustrated by Brian Martin

Publishing Credits

Rachelle Cracchiolo, M.S.Ed., *Publisher*
Conni Medina, M.A.Ed., *Editor in Chief*
Nika Fabienke, Ed.D., *Content Director*
Véronique Bos, *Creative Director*
Shaun N. Bernadou, *Art Director*
Carol Huey-Gatewood, M.A.Ed., *Editor*
Valerie Morales, *Associate Editor*
Kevin Pham, *Graphic Designer*

Image Credits

Illustrated by Brian Martin

5301 Oceanus Drive
Huntington Beach, CA 92649-1030
www.tcmpub.com
ISBN 978-1-6449-1318-5

Table of Contents

I Am Robin Hoodie

Just so you know, I wasn't always a thief. It just kind of…happened. Let me explain.

My name is Zoe Zhang, but my friends call me Zo. We live in a big metropolis called New Hope City, in the colorful Hopping Heights neighborhood on the east side. My family's burrow is snug. Just imagine six cottontail bunnies sharing one bathroom! Still, we love our home.

I spend my days like any ordinary fourth grader. I go to school, do my homework, and help my parents at their bakery. On weekends, I practice soccer and take my three younger siblings to the library. They enjoy adventure stories, just like me.

But when the moon rises and everyone is asleep, I put on my green hood and transform into Robin Hoodie. With my band of Merry Mates, I steal from the greedy and give back to the poor. Like I said, I wasn't always a thief. This is the tale of how I became one.

CHAPTER TWO

Hopping Heights

My life as an outlaw began on a Monday afternoon, about four weeks ago. I took the subway back from school with my five best friends, Bella, Kate, Ary, Kajal, and Maya. We all grew up in Hopping Heights. That day, we headed to my family's bakery, as we normally do. Mom always gives us Chinese pastries to eat while we do our homework.

We passed the corner bodega and waved to Mr. Garcia. He's Maya's dad. He waved back and added more apples to the bin. Ary and Kajal's mom, Mrs. Patel, arranged red roses outside her flower shop across the street. She smiled at us. Bella's grandpa, Mr. Johnson, sat reading on the stoop next door. "Hi, girls!" he called out.

As you can see, people from all backgrounds and cultures live here. It's what makes this place special.

Zhang's Bakery sits near the end of the block. My parents opened it when they first immigrated here. They came to New Hope City with practically nothing and built everything from scratch.

We strolled in, and the heavenly aroma of baked goods instantly filled our noses.

"How was your day, girls?" Mom greeted us. We plopped down at our favorite table by the bay window. A tray of warm taro buns magically appeared before us. They were fresh from the oven.

"Good!" we replied hungrily, each grabbing a golden bun. "Thank you!"

As I chewed, my gaze wandered outside. Mrs. Patel was talking with two guys I hadn't seen before. She seemed nervous, and I saw her hand them a small pouch. *What was in it?* I wondered.

༼༽

I was about to find out. The larger guy stuffed the pouch into his pocket.

Seconds later, the door opened, and they walked into the bakery.

"Do you own this bakery?" the large guy asked Mom.

"Yes, I'm Mrs. Zhang, and this is Mr. Zhang," she said as Dad emerged from the kitchen.

"Ma'am, I'll get straight to the point. I'm John Hornsby, the deputy mayor of New Hope City, and this is Sheriff Joe Cackle," he said gruffly, gesturing to his companion. "I'm in charge while Mayor Richards is away. See, a developer wants to buy your shop. He wants to take over this entire zone. Now, I can prevent this, but it will cost you."

Hornsby's mouth curled into a smirk, and he extended his hand. He wanted money.

My parents looked at each other and motioned to the back. My friends and I exchanged worried glances.

"Our parents work hard for that money," I finally said after a long silence. "We can't let them take it."

"But Zo, what can we do?" asked Kate.

The answer stumped me, but I knew we had to do *something*. I looked at Kate and noticed the book in her hands. It was *The Merry Adventures of Robin Hood*. A lightbulb went off. Robin Hood robbed the rich and gave to the poor. We just needed to break into Hornsby's office and take back the money!

I explained my idea to the girls, and we exchanged excited glances. Robin Hoodie and her squad of Merry Mates were coming to the rescue!

CHAPTER THREE

Wanted!

Over the next two weeks, every time Hornsby and Cackle collected payments from neighborhood shops, we got it back. We nicknamed it Operation: Save Hopping Heights. As soon as night fell, I tossed on my green hoodie and mask, snuck out my bedroom window, and met my friends at the subway.

We rode the train across town to City Hall, where we each had a job. Ary and Kate took the lead, making sure the coast was clear. Kajal, our computer whiz, disabled the alarms. Maya is the smallest. She squeezed under Hornsby's office door to unlock it for us. Bella stood watch in the hallway while the rest of us crept inside.

And me? I used my sharp rabbit hearing to crack the code to the safe, where Hornsby kept the bribes. Then, I swapped the real money with play money.

After every mission, we quietly returned the money to each shop. Our neighbors were overjoyed to get their savings back. But who were these mystery heroes saving the day? Rumblings began to spread of a band of masked avengers. The six of us vowed never to reveal ourselves, and for those few weeks, we thought we had won.

That is, until Hornsby checked his safe and found the fake bills.

"Who stole my money?" Hornsby howled as he and Cackle stormed Hopping Heights. When our neighbors refused to talk, he threatened to let the developer bulldoze the neighborhood. No one budged.

But Hornsby was cunning, too. Calling in the developer meant no more bribe money. He couldn't let thieves outsmart him either. He forced the shop owners to hand over money to him again. Then, he set a trap for us.

ଔ

Hornsby knew we'd break in again, so he and Cackle devised a plan to catch us.

That night, as soon as Maya squeezed under Hornsby's office door

and unlocked it, the two of them leapt out and grabbed her.

"It's a trap!" she squealed, wriggling free.

We fled down the hallway as Hornsby and Cackle gave chase. Fortunately, we had prepared for a moment like this. I grabbed a bag of marbles from my backpack and scattered them behind us. The two crooks collapsed in the hall with a loud *thud*.

We scrambled down the street and into the subway station, just in time to board the next train. When the doors closed, I peered out and saw Hornsby and Cackle running onto the platform. My heart was racing, but I breathed a sigh of relief. We had escaped, for now.

CHAPTER FOUR

Rise and Rise Again

"That was really close," Maya remarked as the train pulled into Hopping Heights station. We nodded glumly.

"Too close," I agreed. We were all rattled. Now that Hornsby had figured out our operation, we needed a new plan. But what? Whatever it was, I knew I had to leave the hood at home this time.

After some much-needed sleep, I called a meeting of the Merry Mates at the bakery. It was a bright and breezy Saturday. All of Hopping Heights seemed to be outdoors enjoying the sun. I watched my neighbors from the bay window, and a feeling of responsibility washed over me. I didn't want to let my friends and family down.

"Does anyone have any ideas?" I asked hopefully, after everyone sat down. I bit into a sweet custard bun and looked around the table.

"Well," Ary began slowly, "I was thinking, our first plan worked because we worked together as a team. What if we made the team…bigger?"

"Do you mean include our neighbors,

too?" I asked. Ary nodded. It made
sense. An entire community standing
up against Hornsby was more powerful
than just the six of us. Still, we also had
to ensure that the greedy developer kept
his paws off our parents' shops. I sighed
for what seemed like the millionth time
in 24 hours. Mayor Richards would
never have let this happen.

My thoughts turned to the story of
Robin Hood. Then, another lightbulb
went off.

"Wait a second," I said. "We need to
get word to Mayor Richards somehow.
We need to show him what's happening
under Hornsby's watch, and I know
exactly how we can do it."

ॐ

We decided it would be best if Robin
Hoodie and the Merry Mates laid
low. For the next few days, we stayed
away from City Hall while Hornsby

and Cackle continued to collect their payments. But here's what they didn't know. *We* had set a trap for *them*.

All week long, we knocked on doors after school. We told our neighbors about our plan and presented them with a petition to sign. It requested that the mayor fire Hornsby and Cackle. But we needed proof of their crimes, too. So, with help, we set up hidden cameras in the shops. When Hornsby and Cackle demanded money, we caught it all on tape.

We put the petition and tapes in a package for Mayor Richards. We sent it off and waited.

Another week passed, but we heard nothing. I grew anxious.

"What if the package got lost?" I asked. "What if Hornsby knows?"

"Stop worrying, Zo," Bella reassured me. "Our plan will work." She's always been the most optimistic of us all, and she's usually right, too.

I heard giggling and turned my attention to my three siblings. They were playing freeze tag behind the counter. I smiled and relaxed a little.

Suddenly, Mr. Garcia burst into the bakery. "Turn on the news!" he cried. "Hornsby and Cackle were arrested this morning!"

Dad flipped on the television. Sure enough, there were New Hope City's deputy mayor and sheriff in handcuffs on the courthouse steps.

Bella was right again. Our plan had worked!

Before we could celebrate, though, the door opened again, and

Mayor Richards walked in with two police officers.

Oh no, I thought, *are we in trouble, too?* We did break the law. He quickly put my fears to rest, however.

"Hello! I understand I owe my thanks to some youngsters here," Mayor Richards roared cheerily. Mom smiled and pointed in our direction.

"Because of your work, we can put Hornsby and Cackle away," he said. "I speak for the citizens of New Hope City in expressing their gratitude."

"Anything to help, sir," I said.

Mayor Richards grinned. "Oh, and if you run into Robin Hoodie and her Merry Mates, tell them I said thank you as well." With a wink, he disappeared out the door.

CHAPTER FIVE

Hanging Up the Hood

So, that's it. That's the tale of how
I became a thief. It's also the story of
how we saved Hopping Heights. After
his return, Mayor Richards made sure
that no greedy developers ever bothered
us again. Hornsby and Cackle went to
jail. Their criminal days were over.

Life for me and my friends went back to normal. We still take the subway home from school. We still wave hello to Mr. Garcia, Mrs. Patel, and Mr. Johnson on our way to the bakery. Mom still greets us with warm taro buns. We still sit in our favorite spot by the bay window.

As for Robin Hoodie, I've hung up my green hood and mask. But if Hopping Heights ever calls again, you can bet that she and the Merry Mates will be ready to answer.

About Us

The Author

Vickie An grew up in Houston, Texas. She's lived and worked in places all over the world, but New York City holds a special place in her heart because of its rich diversity. In her spare time, Vickie enjoys traveling, experiencing new cultures, and trying new foods. Still, there's nothing like a warm Chinese pastry, fresh from the oven—her daughter, Zoe, would agree!

The Illustrator

Brian Martin is an author and illustrator from Richmond, Virginia. As an illustrator, he loves to tell stories with his bright and whimsical art and has illustrated over 30 children's books. He is always looking for opportunities to bring stories to life for both children and parents to enjoy. When he isn't busy writing or making art, he enjoys playing with his four amazing kids.